A Most Unusual Day

by Sydra Mallery · Illustrations by E. B. Goodale

Greenwillow Books, *An Imprint of* HarperCollins *Publishers*

A Most Unusual Day

Text copyright © 2018 by Sydra Mallery

Illustrations copyright © 2018 by E. B. Goodale

All rights reserved. Manufactured in China.

For information address HarperCollins Children's Books,

a division of HarperCollins Publishers, 195 Broadway, New York, NY 10007.

www.harpercollinschildrens.com

The full-color art was painted with black acrylic ink and watercolors, then

digitally collaged with letterpress-printed textures. The text type is Joanna MT.

Library of Congress Cataloging-in-Publication Data is available.

ISBN 978-0-06-236430-2 (hardcover)

18 19 20 21 22 SCP 10 9 8 7 6 5 4 3 2 1

First Edition

Greenwillow Books

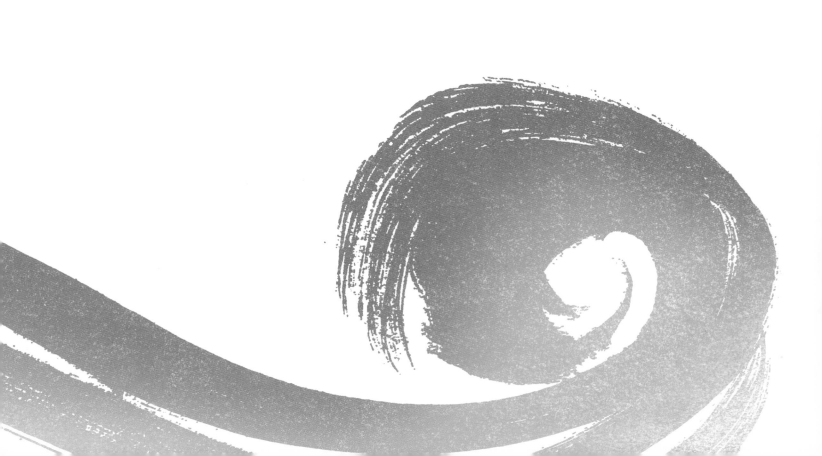

sually, Caroline was awake with the birds.
Her eyes would fly open and she'd jump into
her parents' bed with a morning song for them.

But not today.

Today Caroline lay still in her bed with her eyes closed,
imagining the day before her.

Today would be unusual.

Caroline was usually organized.
But not today.

In her and Grandma's rush to catch the bus
she forgot her socks.
She forgot her lunch box.

Her feet were sweaty and
she had to eat school lunch.

Mohammed Jones offered Caroline
some of his lunch.
"You'll need your strength," he advised.
"That's okay," she said.

But it wasn't.

Not today.

She moved her broccoli across the foam tray

and made a broccoli family: A big, tall mother.

A slightly shorter father. The daughter and one more thing . . .

Caroline was usually graceful.
But not today.

Today, when Ms. Oliver asked,
"What is a family?"
Caroline raised her hand a little too fast,
bumping Wendy Walker by mistake,
on her really-really-loose front tooth
just enough to make it fall out.

Wendy wasn't mad.

"Thanks, Caroline," she said, patting her on the knee.

"I've been waiting for that tooth to fall out."

Caroline smiled, but she felt slightly strange,

like the space where Wendy's tooth once was.

Caroline was usually helpful.
But not today.

Today she wiped the tables.
Well, she tried.

Today she fed the fish.
Well, she tried.

She tried to clean up the art center.
She really tried.

She thought she ought to practice for home.
Dad said they'd be needing her help. Soon.

"You must be tired from all of that helping, Caroline," Ms. Oliver said. "Would you like to come over here and read with us?"

Caroline was usually calm.
But today something kept her tapping her foot,
kept her tilting her chair,
kept her chewing her thumbnail.
She kept thinking about what would happen.
Soon.

She kept looking
at the clock.

Looking
at the door.

Something was unusual about today.

Because at the end of the day, at dismissal,
right when Caroline was unthinkingly,
inexplicably, drawing an airplane
on the school wall with her
"I Got Caught Being Good" pencil—

right when Ms. Oliver looked at her,
and gasped, "Caroline!"—
the bell rang.

Usually, Caroline's parents were calm and collected.
But not today.

Today Daddy's glasses were held together with tape.
Today Mommy's socks did not match.
They had sleepy eyes and big giant smiles.

Today they had a blanket.
Today they had a bundle
from far, far away.

Today they had her new baby sister.

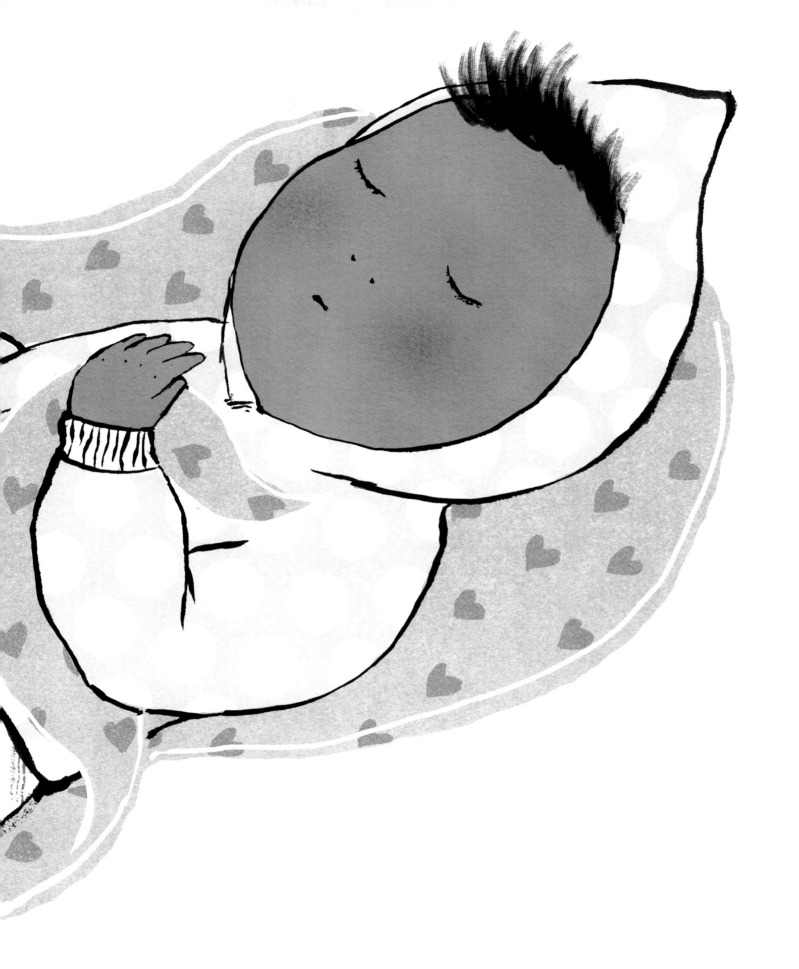

With her toes, perfectly curled
her eyes, perfectly bright
her cry, perfectly high
her fingers—so strong and so, so small—
perfectly tight
around Caroline's finger.

This baby made everything,
every usual thing,

unusually new
and perfectly right.

This baby, her sister, made Caroline's day.